DUMBu

AUTUMN
PUBLISHING

One special day, Mr Stork flew down and landed on the roof of a train carriage. "Oh, Mrs Jumbo! Special delivery for Mrs Jumbo!" he called, hopping from one train carriage to the next.

From one carriage, Mr Stork saw several elephant trunks waving at him. Mr Stork hopped into the train carriage.

"Which one of you ladies is expecting a little bundle of joy?" he asked.

"Right over there," the elephants answered, pointing to Mrs Jumbo. Everyone cooed when the bundle fell open.

"Aaachoo!" the little elephant sneezed. His ears, which had been neatly tucked behind his head, flopped open. They were enormous!

The elephants shrieked with laughter. "Just look at those ears," one elephant giggled. "Why, with those ears, you should call him Dumbo!"

The elephants' teasing made Mrs Jumbo angry. Turning her back on the others, she picked up her baby, carried him to a corner of the train carriage and lay down beside him.

She didn't care if her baby's ears were big. She thought he was beautiful just the way he was. Cuddling him in her trunk, she gently rocked him to sleep.

The next day, the townspeople followed the
parade to the circus ground.
   The Ringmaster called to the gathering crowd,
"Hurry, hurry, hurry! Step right up and get your tickets!"
   In the elephant tent, Mrs Jumbo was quietly bathing
Dumbo when a bunch of rowdy boys ran in.

"Look at those ears!" they shouted when they saw Dumbo.
Laughing and jeering, they pulled the poor elephant's ears.
    Mrs Jumbo wanted to protect her baby, so she picked up a
bale of straw and threw it at the boys to scare them away.
    "Help! Mad elephant!" they screamed.
    The trainers quickly came, dragged Mrs Jumbo away and
locked her up on her own, with chains tied to each of her
four legs.

Dumbo, crying for his mother, thought he had no friends in the world. Even the other elephants turned their backs on him.

But Dumbo was wrong. Someone did want to be his friend.

In a corner of the tent sat a little mouse named Timothy. He had seen and heard everything. When Timothy saw how the other elephants treated Dumbo, it made him mad.

"Look at that poor little fella," the little mouse said. "Everyone's making fun of his ears. What's the matter with them? I think they're cute."

"Aw, you aren't afraid of little old me, are you?" Timothy asked Dumbo, who was hiding. "I'm Timothy Mouse and I'm your friend, Dumbo. I have a plan to help you free your mother."

At that, Dumbo forgot all about being scared.

"I know you're embarrassed by your ears, kid," Timothy said. "But lots of people with big ears are famous. So all we gotta do is make you a big star. But first we need a really colossal act. And I'm just the fellow to think of one."

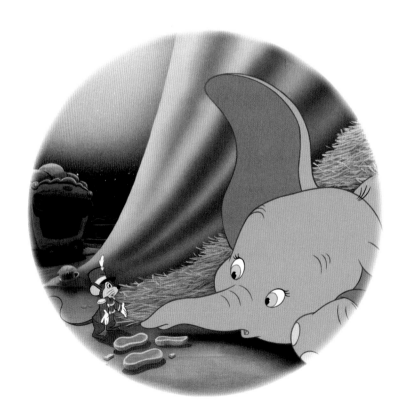

The next day, Timothy had put his plan to make Dumbo a star into action.

The Ringmaster blew his whistle and the first elephant climbed on top of a large ball.

Dumbo and Timothy watched as the pyramid rose higher and higher, until it almost reached the top of the tent.

"And now, ladies and gentlemen," the Ringmaster shouted, "the world's smallest elephant will spring to the top of the pyramid!"

But as Dumbo began his run-up, his knotted ears untied and he stumbled over them, right into the elephant pyramid.

The pyramid teetered and swayed. The crowd ran for their lives as the elephants began to fall.

Trumpeting and bellowing, the elephants tumbled down, crashing into beams and platforms, and pulling down wires and ropes. Finally, they crashed into the centre tent pole.

The enormous tent began to sway and billow. Then, with a huge groan, it collapsed. Dumbo was left sitting alone and unhappy in the middle of the ruins.

The very next show, the clowns painted Dumbo's face and
dressed him as a baby. They put him on a tiny platform high
up in a building surrounded by crackling, make-believe flames.
Dumbo stood shaking with fear, while far below, clowns
dressed as firemen ran around squirting hoses at each other.

"The baby will have to jump!" a clown fireman announced. The rest of the firemen held up a thin safety net.

Closing his eyes, Dumbo leapt from the building. He fell through the net and landed in a tub of wet plaster. The audience roared with laughter.

As the clowns bowed to the cheering crowds, they paid no attention to Dumbo, who crept from the tent feeling hurt, humiliated and miserable.

After the show, the clowns celebrated in their tent. "Cheer up, Dumbo," Timothy said, as he scrubbed his friend's sad little face. "I've found out where they're keeping your mother. I'm going to take you to see her later tonight."

A small smile crossed Dumbo's face. Things wouldn't seem so bad if he could just see his mother.

Later that night, while most of the circus folk slept, Timothy took Dumbo to the wagon where his mother was chained. "Mrs Jumbo, someone to see you!" Timothy called.

Mrs Jumbo put her trunk through the bars of the window and stroked Dumbo's head. She wrapped her trunk around Dumbo and rocked him lovingly.

At last it was time to leave. Tearfully, Dumbo and his mother waved goodbye.

   As Timothy and Dumbo returned to the clowns' tent, they heard the clowns talking about their act. "Let's make the house taller tomorrow!" shouted a clown.
   Dumbo felt sad. He didn't like being laughed at during the clowns' act, and a taller house just sounded scary.
   All Dumbo wanted was to be with his mother. He started to cry. Timothy sat by his side and comforted Dumbo.
   Feeling very tired, Dumbo fell asleep and started to have the strangest dream...

In the dream were
Timothy and Dumbo.
The little elephant was
blowing bubbles from his
trunk. Soon, the bubbles
looked just like elephants –
elephants that danced and
flew all around them both.

The next morning, Timothy tried to convince Dumbo that he could fly. He said Dumbo's ears were so big, they were like wings. He then gave his friend a bird feather, saying it was magical and would help Dumbo. The little elephant wasn't so sure, but he trusted Timothy. With the help of the magic feather, he would try to fly at his next performance.

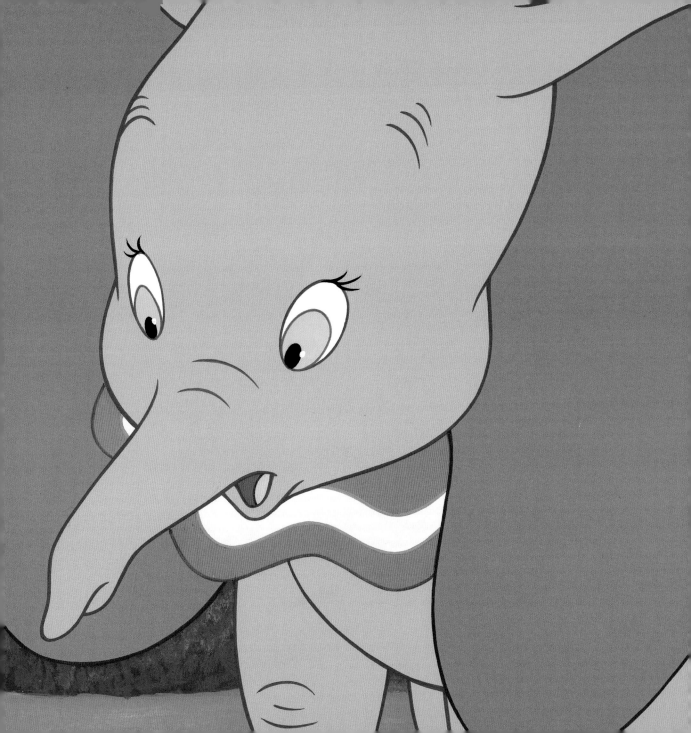

Soon it was time for Dumbo to perform again with the clowns. He stood on the platform with Timothy perched on his trunk. The clowns had built the burning house higher and the ground looked very, very far away.

But this time Dumbo wasn't afraid. He clutched his magic feather in his trunk and waited for his cue.

"Come on, jump! Jump!" the clowns shouted.

Dumbo jumped from the platform. But as they flew through the air, the wind tore the feather from Dumbo's trunk.

Without his magic feather, Dumbo didn't believe he could fly. He and Timothy hurtled towards the ground.

Timothy slid to the end of Dumbo's trunk. "Open your ears and fly!" he pleaded, telling his friend he didn't need the feather. "You can fly all by yourself!"

Dumbo heard Timothy's words and believed them. And what's more, he believed in himself. At the last second, Dumbo spread his ears and he began soaring up and up and up. The astonished audience went wild as Dumbo zoomed after the clowns, chasing them around the ring. The crowd roared as he dived at the Ringmaster. They applauded thunderously as Dumbo did loop-the-loops and rolls and spins in the air.

Dumbo was famous. All the newspapers carried pictures of him and Timothy. Most importantly, Mrs Jumbo was let out of her cage and reunited with her son.

Dumbo thought it was great fun being a star. But what he loved best of all was being with his mother once again.